STEVE ROGERS

EVERY EVIL HAS A DEFINITE BAD END

SAHIL KHAN A

Made with ♥ on the Notion Press Platform
www.notionpress.com

I HAVE DEDICATED THIS BOOK

FOR MY BELOVED FAMILY!!

Contents

Acknowledgements

I will like to show my gratitude to my teachers, principal, my beloved Institute SJRKPS and my parents for the opportunity, support and encouragement from their side. I would like to thank my family and friends for their cooperation and for helping me to write.

THANK YOU

PREFACE

I AM HERE WITH A SUSPENSE MYSTERY THRILLER BOOK.

WHO IS SARAH? HOW IS SHE CONNECTED TO THE DIARY? WHO IS STEVE ROGERS? FROM WHERE HE IS? HOW DID HE COME? IS HE A HERO OR VILLAIN? WHAT IS THE ROLE OF THE DRILLING MACHINE? IS THERE ANY TWIST HERE? WHO IS SI? WHAT HAPPENED TO THE SI? WHY THE DAIRY PLAYS AN IMPORTANT ROLE?

READ THE BOOK TO GET THE ANSWERS.......

PROLOGUE

THE WHOLE STORY REVOLVES AROUND

TWO PERSONS STEVE ROGERS AND SARAH

EACH AND EVERY CHAPTER ARE

INTERCONNECTED

A DARK AND MYSTERIOUS BOOK IS AWAITING

A LOVE STORY IS AWAITING.......

I

DIARY

Every evil has a bad end.

2023,

My name is Sarah Khan I am a student in class 11, I chose the science stream because I love Forensic science and I die to study it. I topped my school with the 98 percentile overall. My loyal friends were happy but few were jealous of my percentile. I never cared about them and I led my life happily. I got every happiness in my life except for my father. My mom said my father died when I was a 2-year-old. I don't remember anything about him but he was a

SI in the police and he died during his last mission. Like him, even I wanted to catch the suspects so I chose forensic science as a study option after my 12th class. Everyone use to call me SI's daughter which used to annoy me but at the same time, I used to feel proud because moreover, my father was a SI. I had mixed opinions about him. I do not talk much about him because that person valued his work more than his family. If he ever cared about us he would not go on that bloody mission. Today he could have been with us, even my mom warned him about it but he never listened which is the sole reason to hate him. I never got a chance to love him I think it was his bad. Few people said he was a coward and few people said he was the hero of the mission. I never cared. My mom Alara Maryam Khan was a housewife but now she is a businesswoman. She is the owner of KHAN Industries. She loves me the most she never let me feel the absence of my father. She takes care of my expenses, studies and everything. I had my school trip back then so needed 3 Thousand bucks. I was hesitant to ask permission. I made up my mind not to go on the trip because I was scared to do so. The next day when I was going to school she gave me the amount and I was astonished. I asked how does she know about this. Sweetly she replied how does she forget about her daughter's happiness? I registered my name and after 2 days I left for the trip. I was living the best moments there meanwhile during dinner, we gathered at the canteen, everyone was playing pick and speak where all shared their experiences. Now it was my turn to speak, with a smile on my face I started walking towards the stage and everyone was excited to hear me. I took a chit and the topic was " My Lovely Father" I was in shock but at the same time I got a chance to get rid of this mysterious part of my life once in all and I announced my topic while returning I heard the voice of few boys who were continuously screaming "Coward! Coward! Coward!" for the first time I stopped and tears broke out. I kneeled down as I was not able to control my tears and I was whispering "Stop! please stop it!" Bilal came and made me stand. He yelled at them and everyone stopped. Then I ran into my room and slept. The next day Bilal came towards me and asked about my mood. We talked to each other and we reached Bangalore. The trip ended and everyone reached home safely. The next day it was my birthday, Bilal called me on my mobile and he invited me for ice cream. I dressed beautifully and I went to the polar bear he arrived with a bouquet. He gave me the bouquet and wished me a happy birthday. We sat and he ordered a Death by Chocolate. A person arrived who was mysteriously dressed, he was wearing a hoodie and he gave me a gift, I was a bit surprised because he was an unknown man. Then he went away, Bilal came and he asked who gave him the book. I said the man wearing a hoodie came and he handover the gift. He said I will open the gift and give it to me! I gave. He opened the gift there was a letter and a diary. In the letter " HAPPY BIRTHDAY SARAH" I was confused, the thing which more shocked me is the owner of the diary is

SAHIL KHAN. It was my father's diary, Bilal was shocked, and I was shocked. I was running high on adrenaline and fell unconscious. When I opened my eyes I was in the hospital. He said that my father is a Hero. I asked him what was the reason for him to say so. He did not say anything but he started to read the diary.....

"

12th November 2005

I am Tanay Mishra a Dentist, I live alone in Anantapur. I want to go on a trip this week to Kullu Manali. I booked a train to Bangalore so I can reach Delhi as soon as possible. I reached Bangalore 2 hours late the time was already 7:30 PM and I had my connecting train to Delhi at 7:45 PM, I was already late and I had to cross 10 platforms to catch my Rajdhani Express so I started to run and just boarded my train and it departed. It was a kind of great relief for me. I went to my seat and the caterer arrived and asked for my meal plan. I ordered a veg meal as I wanted a light dinner. I was having my dinner a sponge ball came and fell into paneer butter masala it was a kid who threw the ball. I was annoyed that time and the kid apologized for his blunder. The kid's father also apologized for the same and he went away I called the caterer and he took back the meal. I took out my favourite book Ignited Minds and I started to read meanwhile the kid's father came and sat in front of me. He first introduced himself his name was Steve Rogers and we started to discuss business and politics. His whole family stayed in Kullu Manali. He ordered me a new meal and I thanked him for the meal. Then he asked me if I was Tanay from Anantpur's Loyal Boys high school. I said yes!! but I was confused that how did he know then he said "I heard you had an accident last year" I did not remember anything because I am a patient with Alzheimer's disorder. So I said yes. He said that he came and met me when I was in a coma. But he was still in doubt that if I was Tanay Mishra. But by now he was confirmed. He was very polite in nature and a well-mannered man. I was happy that I met my childhood friend whom I don't remember. Expect the Unexpected. It was time to sleep, he went and slept and even I fell asleep. The next day when I opened my eyes my train had reached Secunderabad. Unfortunately, my train was running 3 hours late and Steve came with breakfast in his hands. We enjoyed our breakfast with good idly and Wada. His son came and started to play on my mobile I let him play because he was a small kid. A very good bond was built in a few hours. After many days I got a new friend. I was happy indeed and he was too because he had got a childhood friend back. He invited me to his home for lunch. But I denied the offer because I had to reach Leh by tomorrow. The next day we reached Delhi then I took my bus to Manali and said bye to Steve and his family. I gave a chocolate gift box to his son so he was dancing with joy. A short-term meet-up keeps us high, happy and cheerful. It leaves many memories behind that are very beautiful. Then I again slept till my bus reached the ghat section. I wanted to enjoy the curves and the foothills of the Himalayas. The snow, the peaks, the sunset and the sunrise are so fascinating. But life is not so simple it had to take a turn now on the ghat section. A few minutes passed my bus driver fell unconscious and the bus lost its control and boom! the bus fell from a cliff. I was pinned to the glass because of gravitational pull and my cheeks were flattened on the glass and my eyes were widely opened and I was staring down falling to death. I was thinking maybe the area would become haunted by our spirits. Unusual thoughts came to my mind and then I closed my eyes in hope of heaven. I opened my eyes and it was Steve standing in front of me "I asked him that did he even came to heaven?" he said we are on earth. As soon he came to know about the accident he came to save me and he took me to his home. He took me to his home and I had dinner then I slept. The next day when I woke up I noticed there was nobody but only steve. I asked him where is his family. He said I sent them to his mother's house. I was reclining on the chair and Steve was preparing Breakfast. I was thirsty and went into the kitchen and drank water. The next scene stunned me. There was the poison bottle boiling with food. I got to know that something was wrong. Then I came back silently and sat on the chair. He came and took the bottle silently and put it in the dustbin. I said that I have to leave for Manali then he said no without having breakfast I cannot go. Then it flicked me that this guy is mysterious and I said that I have to leave now and I packed my bag and opened the door. Steve said from 20 meters away "Well! well! well! you are a good actor, you never saw the poison bottle?? I saw you in the kitchen and I know you are trying to run away but yeah hear a secret the breakfast is especially for you, by the way, I fed it to a rat last month and it ate so much that it died and I had to dig a tomb for it, so will you try this?" I got to know that he is a psych and I thought to run but he threw a hammer and luckily I dodged it and ran into a room and locked the door. I was in shock and closed my eyes tightly. After a few seconds, I opened my eyes and I was stunned again. The atmosphere of the room was creepy. Walls were stained by blood and flies were all over the room. There was a bed which was made up of iron and it was too rusted, the smell was spread and freezers were running. He was banging on the door continuously and screaming my name. I became still and sat in the corner and he was still banging. It became harder when he banged a knife which came through the door. He stopped banging. Then he started laughing so hard that his vocal cord would come out. Then he started to speak, he said me to open the freezers because a surprise was waiting for me. I made myself fit and stood up. I went and opened the freezers and it was a nightmare for me to open. There was a dead body chopped and the ice cubes inside turned red. I could not resist it so I vomited out and because of no food blood even came out. It was a jail for me. I took a metal rod and opened the door slowly. Luckily, he was not there. I dashed towards the door. But a hammer hit my head. I felt lifeless and fell. I cleared my eyes and I was sitting on a chair and was tied to it by strings. I was in a big warehouse. A man wearing a black hoodie and a mask came and stood. He was holding a drill in his hand. He unwrapped his face. It was Steve. I inquired why you are committing this. He said " You are asking this, hahaha a psycho is asking this. You would have thought about what could arise after killing Lauren. I was the one who gave my sister's hand to you despite knowing that you are a psycho. Now it's time for revenge!!" Within seconds, he took the drilling machine and drilled it into my skull.

15th OCTOBER 2006

John sir said " Very well executed documentary SI sahil khan, very precisely done with the short story and the way you have collected the information about how Steve kills the suspects and investigation and assumption in Tanay Mishra murder case is excellently presented"

I thanked him and returned home. My wife and my daughter Sarah were waiting for me at home. As it was Sunday Alara cooked biriyani for me. I had to take a new toy for Sarah today so I left the office early today.

END OF CHAPTER I

II

SIR

18th November 2006

It was heavily raining. That night, the power abruptly got cut. "knock knock" the shrill tone hit my ears and I checked who it was. They were Pavan and Rahul. They said, "Sir, you have to come back to Bangalore, this case is very intricate and identically killed. We need you, sir, we have to solve this case as soon as possible". I asked Alara to pack my bag and went to Bangalore.

I reached Bangalore in the morning and came home. I became fresh and wore my khaki. I prepared my breakfast and ate it. I sat on my bike, a classic 350. The sound from my bike Silencer always attracted children to my layout. They always ran behind it to the main road. I stopped near a tea stall where I always drink tea and reached the police station. I saw Rahul coming towards me and he further said " Good morning sir, we have found the prime suspect and the prime suspect is in the investigation room. Please start, it is very complicated and it seems Bangalore got a new Serial killer. He needs to stop otherwise Blood is going to rain instead of water, It's the first time in 12 Decades so many dead bodies have been found. We do not need the past to come on and John sir is on the investigation with the NHAI and you can begin your investigation, sir". I appeared inside full of frustration and sat on the chair he was sleeping. I banged on the table, but he did not get up and I did the same so he did not wake up again. My frustration came out as an explosion, my left hand hit hard on his face and he woke up in shock and started to cry like a small child. I was regretting that I had unnecessarily beaten him. I gave a water bottle to him and he drank it within seconds as if he hadn't eaten anything or drunk water. So I thought to conduct myself politely with him and take the investigation softly. I waited for a few minutes and asked "Why are you crying? ". He said"What did I do sir? Why I am here?" I said " You are here because you were driving the truck in which there were 7 dead bodies that too they are brutally murdered, Now without wasting my time tell me the reason you killed them or why you brought them here?" He said"Sir please listen to me, I did not kill anyone. I didn't know that there were dead bodies in the truck". I said " I am not a fool to hear your nonsense now". He furthermore said"

Sir, there are two options one who takes poisonous candy and one who sells that candy. Who is wrong here? I belong to a poor background sir I did not do anything sir please leave me, my daughter is going to get married tomorrow please sir" I said. "tell me the truth". He said "Sir, I have two daughters and they are twins. I fixed their marriage the same day and I wanted money for the reception. So I asked my boss. He said that I should go to Bangalore and dump the truck and don't even dare to open it and you will be earning 2 Lakhs for this, that's why I did sir pls let go of me". I said "I can't believe you, you have to stay in prison till it is solved " he was begging me to leave him, but it was my duty. The inquiry proceeded and I went home. My mobile started vibrating and it was Rahul who had called me and said, "Good afternoon sir, we have found another truck with two dead bodies and 3 members in it". The situation was getting out of control and something had to be done so I dashed towards the police station. While Bangalore was getting out of control, darkness had already covered Bangalore and crime was unstoppable. I was freaking out every bloody moment. I had not come across anything like this and I arrived police station and John sir was waiting for me. I met him, I never saw him so tense till now. He wanted to catch the killer and he said that the truck owner we were searching for is dead now. The owner was found in the 2nd truck. Now the only suspects were the truck driver and the 3 members found in the 2nd truck. Now the game of brutal investigation had to begin. I called one by one to the investigation room and the first suspect was Raman. I asked him why he was in the truck. He said " I work in a warehouse present in Anantapur and a man wearing a black hoodie came with a screwdriver in his hand and he killed them. We three begged for our life so he dragged us into the truck with the dead bodies and locked us in that was the last thing we noticed about him and it was very difficult for us to survive a night with dead bodies. Sir, please arrange food, we have not eaten anything in 24 hours". Then I called the driver who was driving the second truck he too gave the same answer to me. Then I called Raghav and as expected they gave the same answer. Then I called John sir and said about the investigation and arranged the suspects' food. Then I again went to my home and took some rest.

It was twilight already. John sir called me and said that the post-mortem report was ripe. So he called me to his residence. I was tired but sir had ordered I had to go to his home. I went to his home by my car and I reached on time and Sir and the doctor were already waiting for me. As soon as I reached the doctor started to explain the report. Consultant " Sir, it was easy to denote the cause of death. The casualties were because of drilling into their skulls." Pawan entered and he kept listening to us. The doctor said that the patients were suffering from Alzheimer's disorder. Sir asked him for the feast but he refused and he left. I was in shock that how could all be Alzheimer's disorder but I had got clear info that it was Steve because it was the pattern used by Steve Rogers. Pawan said"Sir, we have to leave for Ananthapur. We have got the warehouse address Presumes he will be attending there." After dinner, John sir took us and left for the same. We did a journey overnight and we reached there. It was 7 in the morning and the warehouse was vacant with a creepy look. Only a few trucks were resting in peace. The deteriorating smell was dissipated all over because the plasma of humans was spread. This indicated the brutality of Steve. We checked the proprietor of the godown and we were sick because the person we were checking was in our custody. What a game the man played with us. Then John sir was shocked and he was very eager to catch Steve, he said we have to rush to Bangalore as soon as possible.

We rushed towards Bangalore and there was heavy traffic that day because it was the weekend and we reached the police station late, John sir just crashed into the prison and dragged Raman mercilessly into the investigation cabin. He slapped him so hard, we were shocked to see his anger. That was the most brutal look of John sir and he said "Wow Steve, wow you believed that you would never be apprehended. You are wrong now. Tell me the truth." He was laughing and he kicked him and slapped him again. After a while, he uttered a word. It was the name "Michael".

Present-day,

My dad's diary stated his role and the problems he faced during the investigation. I was hearing his story with full of Interest, my mom came and Bilal had to stop. She first asked me, who is Bilal and why are we in the hospital, I explained the whole thing to her. She paid the hospital bills and thanked Bilal for helping me and taking care. She took me back home but I needed to complete the diary. I was shocked to know about that killer Steve, How brutal he was and how my dad faced him? The next day when I went to school I asked Bilal to narrate the next part of the story. Unfortunately, there were no free periods today so I said let us bunk the classes. He was I have gone mad. But I wanted to continue the diary at any cost. Then we planned and bunked the class and finally, we did it. We went to a library and sat. Then Bilal started to read.........

End of Chapter II

III

MICHAEL

We asked Steve who is Michael and why he took his name? so he said that they killed him but I wanted to kill them...

Steve's backstory.....

It was heavily raining. The water was rushing into the roads. I saw a basket flowing with water. Everything was dim but on the white cloth, I could see and hear a baby, it was weeping. In a fraction of a moment, I ran and grabbed it and came home. My father was happy because a saved a life. But I never thought that the small life I saved would be my partner in crime also known as my brother. We grew up and we loved him too much. It was confidential that he was adopted. He grew up and

my parents shifted to Sydney because of my dad's transfer. He said that he is going to a friend's birthday celebration. But I never knew that It was our last symposium. I went to the police station and registered a grievance. My mom and dad came back from Sydney. I was called to the police station. They presented a dead body and removed the cloth. My tears broke out and the land between my legs broke down. I was numb and silently came out and the rain started I crouched down and cried and screamed. Screaming in the pain of losing a gem. The police said it was an accident.

I couldn't believe it. So I started to enquire again on my own. When I asked Michael's friends they said that he did not even attend the gathering. I checked the CCTV and saw that some goons took him with them. I found them. Took a hammer and hit them they fell lifeless and I took them with me and tied them to a chair. They woke up and started to tell" Sir why are you doing this what we have done to you?" "Tell me why did you kill Michael?" They said" We

are suffering from Alzheimer's disease. Our greatest concern broke out we lost our way home. We searched but we never got it. The weather was so drowsing and we were crying on the footpath. A jeep reached, and a man holding a half-used cigar got down his hair was long, and he had a gun in his pocket he was the same as a human demon. He said will u come with me? and we said yes because we had not had any other option. He gave us good clothes and food and a home. He was our saviour. One day he called us and said do as he says. we agreed with him. He made us rob and murder. We were completely his serve as. One day we tried to rob your brother. But he did not have anything, we took him with us and tortured and kill him. We threw him on the tracks that it would plot as an accident." I was frustrated and took

a drilling machine drilled many times and killed that bleed to death.

END OF STEVE'S BACK STORY

After listening to Steve we were broke emotionally and at the same time, I was angry because what we did was wrong. However, tomorrow was a trial session in court. So I kept quiet. The very next day we headed to court and reached it but without Steve. The magistrate asked us where is steve. "Dear sir we are so sorry that Steve is not present with us at this moment because someone called us and said to change our route because somebody was waiting to rescue Steve. But we were trapped in our other route, someone threw the eggs on the windshield and took the accused with them". After this, we're suspended for 6 months on account of the act of carelessness.

8 months later,

I joined duty 2 months back and started the investigation about Steve. I sent Rahul Ananthapur to the warehouse to trace some clues. He called me "Good afternoon sir, we have found Steve but not alive. He has been kept in freezers for months and has been drilled many times and his all blood is drained. And very cruelly murdered. We found a letter with it".

The Letter,
"Every evil has a Definite bad end"

Present day,

So Steve was finally dead and what a cruel person he was and at the same time felt bad for poor Michael and here Steve's chapter came to an end. But who killed steve? and why? Bilal said now the story was going to change totally and I was excited to know. But the bell rang and it was Maths class so I did not want to miss it and we left for the class. Police life is not like the way we think and I got to know how my father was restless in his work. They

are very hardworking and dedicated to their work. Then I went to the mall and enjoyed myself there with my friends we planned a two-day outing and luckily Mom agreed to the outing. We departed to Puducherry.....

End of Chapter III

IV

STEVE

The next day we arrived at Puducherry and we went to the hotel and booked 3 rooms and we left for the beach. The beach was amazing neat and clean. We took out our barbeque and we took some amazing fish and Rohan and Sanjana cleaned the fish and we got our fish and I settled them on the hot barbeque and we enjoyed the dinner and came back to our hotel. Now I had to know what happened next in my dad's life. I was tired and I was not able to read and again I had to call Bilal for reading. I called him and he started to read the diary.........

Who was the killer? Why was Steve killed? He was a psycho who could kill him. We solved a riddle but it left another behind it. It was the worst thing about the case. I am not able to sleep for a while for the last 8 months. Whenever I close my eyes I get a portrait of the dead Steve. It makes me open my eyes forcefully. Anyways tomorrow I will be in Ananthapur for a proper investigation. Where and when the game commenced I had to expire it there. By the way, I was under John sir I reported him the next day and left for Ananthapur in my car.

I reached the godown first. I was so creepy as no one dared to go there. I searched the whole. But no clues. I took my car for heading back to Bangalore but, I saw a CCTV system. I got down and rushed towards the office and turned on the monitor and checked the CCTV footage. I that it was clear that Steve was not alone a man wearing a black hoodie and face mask was on. It was dated 15th November. They brought a man inside and a truck left the godown. The truck we caught after a while another truck left, and it was also caught. Then a man who they took inside was that who was found in the truck dead he was not the owner. Wait what the owner is Steve Roggers? The firm's name is Lauren co limited. They went to Ananthapur

railway station. And a went there and again checked the CCTV they were seen boarding Mysore Express in coach B4. Only the black hoodie person boarded and I checked the passenger list only one was travelling to Mysore. I was out of my word because the passenger was John sir. He was travelling to Mysore his hometown. I took my car and headed to Mysore. Checked the footage there I

*saw John sir getting down
and no other got down. He was holding the suitcase which was with the hoodie person. I sat in my car and started to think how sahil sir was there and he knows something about the case. Something he knows. He is connected to this. Is the killer of steve. Let me check by reaching his home.*

*I arrived at John Sir's home and saw the nameplate "Lauren mansion" and I knocked on the door he opened, it and called me in he
said wait I will prepare coffee and he went inside. I checked the house and saw a black hoodie and a mask. It was ascertained that John Sir was that black hoodie guy. He came and said it was still being prepared and I asked sir which is your hometown he said that" It's Mysore" again. I asked what were you doing in Ananthapur on 15th November? He said I was in Mysore. I again said sir don't lie sir I saw you entering the train and getting down in Mysore and what is that black hoodie. He said wait I will come and tell.*

He brought coffee and offered a big cup but I wanted a small one because I was not in the mood. I asked for the small one he refused, he was forcing me to drink the big one, I thought something is wrong and an agreement began and it into a fight. I just kicked him and forced him and I fed him the coffee forcefully. I went on and sat on a chair to control my breadth and he stood holding a hammer. I was sitting and he came in front of me he made an action to hit me but fell because of the so-called coffee. I tied him to a chair. He was asleep. I checked the room. There were images of victims who died and there was a picture of a lady. He woke up and started to call me and he was laughing he said" You got to know who I am, " I asked him who are you? He uttered a word

"STEVE ROGGERS "

Present day,

No words had left in my mouth. It was like heartbreak for me to see a respected person as a criminal and I got to know thrilling my dad's life was. He could have died but he survived because of his bravery. Bilal was happy and I was too. Then it was getting more interesting and interesting then I wanted to know what happened next. But it was too late if my friends saw me with Bilal they would start making fun and rumours. Moreover, he was my best friend, I did not want to lose a best friend so I thought to evacuate the place. He went to his room and I too went then slept. I was too eager to know what happened next. It was the biggest twist I ever saw and then sad because my dad was going to die there. Still, the reason he was called a coward was mysterious. I thought I can find the reason in the book. The next day I woke up and became fresh, we planned to have breakfast in a French-style restaurant and we departed. We had to reach Fortshire as soon as possible because we had trained at 4 PM and then we had and then we were walking on the road. We were urgent as we were already late as per the plan. Then we gangsters fighting near the Fortshire and we stopped. We planned we can enter the fort by using another gate. Bilal warned us to do so but did a mistake by choosing the other gate. The backup gangsters were hiding there. When I entered the gate, they saw us and they placed the gun towards us and we were caught by them. We asked them to let us go but they both did not let us. After the war ended the goons came and tied a blind strip to our eyes and tied our hands. They took us to their base and removed our blind strips. Their base was made up of stones and it was looking like an old fort. I got to know that we werenot alone there. A man was also trapped with us. His face was covered with a monkey cap and he was tied to the chair. We begged them to show mercy and leave us but they did not listen to us. The man was next to us and he whispered to Bilal to try to chew the rope and cut it. Bilal refused to do it because he was scared. Again he said to do and he said to trust him. So slowly Bilal started to chew the rope. Bilal hid behind the chair and he was continuing the task. After 25 minutes one of the gangsters came and said that we will be dying today. We got scared and we screamed a loud. Then the man got up as soon as Bilal chewed the rope and he held the goon's hand and snatched the gun. Then he kicked and shot him dead. Slowly other goons entered and he started to fight with them and he kicked one and he shot one. He was fighting like a hero and hope emerged and he continued it. He killed a total of 17 goons and everyone was dead. He turned towards us and started to remove the cap but other fellow goons and he hid and shot one of them. One dragged me and placed the gun on my head and eventually the man had to stop fighting. I screamed because of fear. He said to be quiet otherwise I will be the first to die. I stopped and started to look at the man. His eyes were full of rage and he was staring at the goon who was holding my hair tight. Within blinks, he shot the goon and I fell. He killed the other one. It was like a soldier saving us, a hero saving us. I went towards my friend and removed the ropes and he was looking at me as if he saw me after many years. My friends were free. I asked the man to open his monkey cap. He opened the cap. White shiny beard and a middle-aged man with very less wrinkles, his eyes were brown and tears were breaking out. He was looking at me as a father who is emotional and looking at his daughter. Yes, he was my father.

END OF CHAPTER IV

V

A LOVE STORY....

As soon as I saw him, It was impossible to see him alive and I called him " abba" and I broke down and I fainted. The very next I opened my eyes I was in my hotel room. Everyone was sitting and waiting for me to wake up. Bilal asked how am I feeling now? I said I am okay. Then Vivaan asked, " Sarah, Bilal did not inform you about this earlier?" I was shocked to know that Bilal knew about this. The worst thing was that I was unaware and that Bilal hid this. I got emotional and started to hit him. Vivaan stopped me. I yelled, " Where is Abba?" I kept shouting that and I was crying. Bilal made me calm down and I stopped crying. He said that he went to clear evidence about the fight and I said I have to meet him but Bilal said you take a rest and he will come. I asked him to read the diary from where we ended. He said you take rest but I wanted to know the mystery. So I forced him to read the book. He started to read ....

I was not surprised about John Sir being Steve because he had left many hints and I got to know in the investigation as though that was a shock too because now it was getting difficult for people. Finally, I had got Steve and I wanted to kill him as soon as I find Steve but John sir was Steve. I wanted to know the reason why so much ruckus was created and every serial killer has a story behind it. I asked him" Why you did this Steve?" He said "Steve!! will you not call me Sir? " I said, "Now it's no use to give you respect steve and kindly tell me the reason otherwise no one can find your

burned ash also".

STEVE's FLASHBACK...

I lived in Ananthapur for my studies and my hometown is Mysore. I was studying forensic science. And all my friends were so supportive and helped me. I helped them. Everybody praised me because I had a better IQ than others. One day a girl named Lauren appeared in my life. We were friends and one day her friends said that she likes me. I took it lightly and kept to myself. But after this, I started to observe her more near me.

The rumour was spread that we are couples. I couldn't tolerate her anymore. I called her and warned her to stay away from me. Then she disappeared from the University. It was 20 days since I saw her. I asked about her friends. Her friends said that she is sad and she is at home. They even said what I did was not right she loved me truly. I was feeling guilty. One day I and my friends went shopping. They asked

why are u sleeping late and are so dizzy nowadays. I said nothing I just have guilt for Lauren and like I have started to notice her more but I haven't seen her. They said you have got a disease bro. I asked what type of illness that don't know. They teased me and said, Love. I blushed and rushed to the hostel. I was lying on the bed and thought about it. Was I really in love with her? Yes, my heart said.

Luckily the very next day, she started to come university. I thought to gift a rose and ask sorry.

The next day with rose I went with a rose. She was in the cafeteria. A man came with a rose and gifted her a rose. She took it and I didn't know why my left eye started to water and tears came out. I headed back and I heard my name "John! John!". It was Lauren. She came near me. She said that she had been to her hometown and she said sorry for the

past. She threw the rose in the dustbin. I asked why you didn't like the rose Sameer gave you. She said that he was back of her since her school days. I served glad. I presented the rose and asked sorry and expressed all my feelings. She was dancing with joy and agreed with me. We were comfortable couples. Helped each other in one or the other activities. We topped our semester exams. It was her birthday

the next day. She invited me to her home. I went and explored her house. She was a tea lover and she went to prepare the tea. I was glancing at each and everything I opened the cupboard one side was full of letters. I opened and surveyed the letters. They were love letters. I had not sent any of them. My feeling broke out. She was betraying me. Was she taking vindication that I scolded her?

Numerous horrible thoughts I thought. She came I was sitting impassively. She said your masala tea is ready. I threw the letters on her face. She said that she is holding tea. She kept the tray aside. And she said to tell what I have to tell. I said who gave you these letters. She said "Oh mad did you forget? You were the one who gave these letters. Made me mad at you." I said "What are you telling me? Lauren I never sent anything. I fell in love before the semester exams. You betrayed me. If you had to betray you could have done it before." She broke into pieces. She started to cry. I took the teacup and threw and it broke. I said "Now if you join these broken pieces. It will join but the cracks will be visible. Now it applies to me, Ms Lauren." Without uttering a word I left her house she was crying and following. She was begging for me. I went out and a postman reached me and gave me the letter. It triggered me more. I threw the letter towards her and left for the house.

The very next I got up and turned on the news. I was terrified. Lauren was kidnapped. The police siren was heard. The cars approached me. They said they have take my statements. So I went there and they were acting as if I kidnapped her. By then I did not care. I explained everything to them. But still, they were suspicious. They gave me a letter which the postman gave me yesterday.

The letter

"Hello, buddies how was my game? And everybody got trapped. I know that this letter is read by the police. Now without uttering a phrase give it to Lauren's so-called boyfriend Sahil.

Hey buddy you are so an informed and possessive

lover. By the way, the letters were sent by me. Now It's clear that I have abducted her. If you bring the police to rescue Lauren she will be killed. So you come alone with 1 crore. I forget to tell you that you have to come near pocket hills. "

I was tense about where I had to bring 1 crore and why the hell did scold her. I was a fool that scold her.

I did not even think about her feelings. I took an empty suitcase and did as he said. I reached Pocket Hills. There was a tea shop and a small boy approached me. He gave me a tea cutting and a gift box. I drank the tea and opened the box. There were Lauren's thumbnails. I was stunned and I threw and I did even vomiting. I was crying. That boy said me to climb to the top. When I was climbing I fell

unconscious because the sedative was mixed with tea. I woke up and I saw Lauren beside me. The suitcase was with the guy who had kidnapped us. He was asleep. I thought he did not open the briefcase. Somehow I managed to open my hands and I opened Lauren's ropes and she woke up. She stood straight and I supported her and started to move quietly. We moved half away and she was thanking me for saving her. We both were moving and a bullet hits her. She takes a long breath. She falls into my arms, blood was flowing. Subconsciously she said "Protect me if not the girls who are being targeted, I don't know if I will be alive or not please protect them" With shortness of breath I said, "Lauren please be awake first I will protect you... please be awake" She slowly closed her eyes. It started showering. She was not opening her eyes and I was crying. After a lot of tries, she did not open her eyes. I left her on the floor and turned back. It was the guy who gave the rose to Lauren in the cafeteria. He was the kidnapper. He was 100 meters far from me. I started to run in anger, With Every step, I ran forward my anger increased and at the same time I was getting emotional screaming hard and running in pain I took a sharp log and I lifted my hand to throw it but he shot another bullet it hit my chest I fell on the ground, the whole incidents which took place when I met lauren and the beautiful journey was flashing through my mind. I thought I was going to die but I saw him running away and an ambulance and police jeep arrived.

I opened my eyes I was in the hospital the police rescued me. I asked," Where is Lauren?" They said that I go and rest and I did not I forced them they did not let Lauren be lying on a bed. I was happy and she was sleeping in peace. But I noticed the monitor, it
was blank. I tried to wake her up and she was not even shaking a bit. I got to know she left me. I was crying loudly and loudly. The doctors came and held me and dragged me to the bed. They injected me with a sedative and I slept. Her family came and collected her body. The last glimpse of lauren. A few days passed I was sent home. I was guilty and

depressed. But the kidnapper was not caught. Then I understood keeping quiet is not enough. Lauren will be at peace after I kill him. I got the address of the kidnapper. I broke his house door and rushed inside and came into his room. The wall was full of maps and pictures of girls. He came inside and he fought with me. And I almost killed him he said" I trapped the girls because money, money man, money matters. I killed them after my work was completed the same as Lauren's death." I got emotionally triggered and took a drilling machine and killed the bloody kidnapper. This changed my life. Womanhood needed a hero. After this, I searched for the frauds and started to kill them without a clue and joined the police. So no one can doubt me. One of the doctors became my friend and helped to generate the fake post-mortem report. Luckily the last man I killed had Alzheimer's disease. I hired persons who can act as killers. I needed a name for covering up the murders and here the hero Born.

"STEVE ROGGERS"

End of Steve's back story

Present day 2023,

Love is a drug Steve and many people fall for it and ruin their life. Steve justified true love exists. But what he did was in a wrong manner. Then entered my dad. I left my bed and stood, then I ran to him and gave him a tight hug and started crying. He even kept crying by seeing and then he took my name " It was the most beautiful feeling in the world". Then I asked how was he alive? if he is alive why did he stay away from us? Hiding?

END OF CHAPTER V

VI

THE BEGINNING

He asked till where I completed his diary. I said till love story!! Then he continued......

John sir shocked me by telling his story. I left him alone and took my car and started to head towards the police station. I was thinking was he a hero or villain? I was confused about it. I reached home first before the police station. While taking a shower I thought about the girls who have been trapped like Lauren. Then it reflected that I had to support sahil sir. Then I took my car and headed back to Lauren Mansion. Then I removed the ropes I tied to sahil, sir. He said," Informed in the police station huh?" I said no. Again he asked "Why? Oh, sincerely don't want justice by arresting a Villain?" I said sir let's rescue girls together.
He said," You are a real-life hero and you need not

turn into a fantasy hero." I said sir let's do it. He smiled towards me and " ok your wish". He said our following target is Rahul. He was our colleague. Steve said," He killed 3 girls by this trap" I was stunned and kept listening. Now I was ready to face everything that gonna come up. We called him for dinner at Steve's house. He came we mixed a sedative with food. So he fell
unconscious. We tied him to the chair. John sir's tradition. He wore a black hoodie and a face mask. He had another pair so even I wore it. I said I will kill him. He said, "Then I will not come in you and kill him and return." I went inside and he woke up I removed my mask. He was shocked. I said what he did with the girls. He was laughing and said" u will kill me?? Hahaha" and he opened his ropes and stood erect in
front of me. The drilling machine was not working. He pushed me in anger. I again slapped him and continuously punched him. But it did not work. He again kicked me. It wounded me. He connected the unplugged drilling machine and headed towards me. I left all hope and just said "EVERY EVIL HAS A DEFINITE BAD END"

Steve entered and kicked him so he dashed to the walls. A sight of joy arose. He took a chair and hit him. It broke and he was still unstoppable. I was bleeding from my mouth. However, I managed to get up. With his hands, he started to squeeze sahil sir's throat. There was no alternative so I took the gun and shot Rahul dead. Sahil sir stood and said,"

Good job, by the way, thank you". It was the time. Another bullet got fired from my gun which hit Steve's abdomen. He fell. I went near him and sat I wiped my gun and kept it in his hand. I said Steve or John sir what shall I call you? Ok, Mr Roggerss fine I will tell my opinion. There is my rule if we are doing the right work we have to do it in the right manner or the wrong work in the wrong manner. I did not want to do the right work in the wrong manner." He died. A hero died "Sahil sir" and a villain died"Steve Roggers". But goodwill won over evil. But I had forgotten that John sir was a senior Officer and Rahul was an officer. They both were still innocent in front of the world and only I knew that they were criminals. I would have been caught now. I had no damn idea now. So I thought of running away and vanishing from the world and my family see no effect on me in society. I knew I had done a wrong thing by running away but I wanted to see my family safe. Especially my daughter. I kept my eyes on you Sarah. I had all your information Sarah and Bilal I know him since his childhood and he too knew me. He kept this secret because I had said him. I couldn't tell that I ran because you were small and I waited because when you will grow up, you will be more mature and understand this properly.

Done with a flashback,

I was happy that I got my father back. But now I had to take him back to Bangalore and tell Mom. The next day we reached Bangalore. I and dad reached home. My mom opened the door she was extremely shocked to see SI Sahil Khan alive. She broke into tears and she welcomed him by making a dua. We three kept our right leg and we entered the house. Then we started to live our life happily and many asked where was he. we just made some reason and led our life. One day I saw many bullet marks on his back and many cut marks. I was shocked and yes where was he all the 15 years? How did he survive all these days? and where is his 6th finger? Is he Sahil khan?!!!!!

"EVERY EVIL HAS A DEFINITE BAD END"

END OF STEVE ROGERSVOLUME 1

SURPRISE?

Thank you for reading my first book, your love and support plus encouragement will make the book succeed and
expect a stronger sequel, yes I am returning with Volume 2 soon.......

and the sequel will take us to a new world and it will be a chartbuster. Who will play the lead role? Stay tuned for updates.

- Sahil khan A

9 798890 260543

Printed by Libri Plureos GmbH in Hamburg, Germany